DRAGON
GAMES

THE
THUNDER
EGG

DRAGON GAMES

GAMES

THE THUNDER EGG

BY MADDY MARA

SCHOLASTIC INC.

Copyright © 2023 by Maddy Mara
Illustrations by James Claridades, copyright © 2023 by Scholastic Inc.

All rights reserved. Published by Scholastic Inc., *Publishers since 1920*. SCHOLASTIC and associated logos are trademarks and/or registered trademarks of Scholastic Inc.

The publisher does not have any control over and does not assume any responsibility for author or third-party websites or their content.

No part of this publication may be reproduced, stored in a retrieval system, or transmitted in any form or by any means, electronic, mechanical, photocopying, recording, or otherwise, without written permission of the publisher. For information regarding permission, write to Scholastic Inc., Attention: Permissions Department, 557 Broadway, New York, NY 10012.

This book is a work of fiction. Names, characters, places, and incidents are either the product of the author's imagination or are used fictitiously, and any resemblance to actual persons, living or dead, business establishments, events, or locales is entirely coincidental.

ISBN 978-1-338-85194-6

10 9 8 7 6 5 4 3 2   23 24 25 26 27

Printed in the U.S.A.   40

First printing 2023

Book design by Stephanie Yang

Lunchtime had arrived, but Luca was still in class. He had never been asked to stay back before. He didn't know why he had been asked to stay back today. Luca wasn't perfect, but he didn't usually get into trouble.

On the blackboard, someone had scrawled a weird drawing. There was a shape that looked a bit like a crown. Another looked like a tooth. To the side was something that looked like a fork. Around them all was a squiggly line. Luca was pretty sure Ms. Long had drawn it. But why? And what did it mean?

Ms. Long always did things her own way. Other kids learned English in English class. In history, they did history. Ms. Long's classes weren't like that. In English, they might learn about riddles or codes. In history, they might learn how to make arrows by chipping away at flint.

If Ms. Long could crack your code in less than five minutes, she would rip it up. If the tip of your arrow was not sharp enough to pierce thick cloth, she would toss the whole thing in the trash.

Lots of kids didn't like Ms. Long. They called

her "The Dragon." Some kids swore they'd seen smoke curl from her nostrils when she was upset.

But Luca thought she was interesting. He especially liked her stories. When she was in a good mood, Ms. Long told tales about an imaginary land called Imperia. Maybe she was writing a book or something? Luca didn't know and he didn't care. The stories were cool. Imperia had once been a beautiful place, filled with majestic mountains, endless forests, and ancient cities that shone like gold. That was back when dragons were in charge.

But dark times had fallen on the realm. There were no dragons left. The land was overrun with wild beasts and ruled by a power-hungry leader named Dartsmith. Ms. Long's Imperia stories always ended the same way.

"Only when the three dragons return will Imperia have peace again."

Luca looked back at the chalk drawing on the board. None of the other classrooms had blackboards. But Ms. Long's room was old-fashioned. One wall was completely covered with old display cases. These were made of carved wood and stained glass. Inside them were the sort of things you might find in a museum. Old bones. Strange objects. Rocks.

Weirdly, it was the three rocks that always drew Luca's attention. One rock in particular, the one in the cabinet at the back of the classroom. It was the size and shape of a football.

Once, when she'd been in a surprisingly chatty mood, Ms. Long had taken it out of the cabinet.

"This is a geode," she had said, walking between the tables so everyone could see it up close. "Also known as a Thunder Egg. They are very rare. Thunder Eggs look boring on the outside, but on the inside most of them are crystal. This one, however, is filled with something even more precious."

Luca wanted to touch the Thunder Egg. He felt like the rock was calling to him. But there was no chance. Ms. Long returned it to the cabinet, locking it with her key.

Her good mood disappeared, and she frowned at the class. "If any of you mess with this specimen," she said, "you will enter *a whole world* of trouble."

Now, sitting in the classroom waiting for Ms. Long to appear, Luca stared at the drawing. He stared so hard his eyes started to blur. The lines changed color. Suddenly, they looked gold and not white at all.

"This is a total waste of time," snarled a voice.

Luca started. He'd forgotten he wasn't the only kid asked to stay back during lunch. He turned to look at Zane, the class football champ. Zane's face was scrunched up and he was drumming his pencil on the table.

Ms. Long would have bitten his head off if she'd been around.

"Wow! Zane, you look *soooo* amazing right now."

This comment came from the third kid asked to stay back that afternoon. Yazmine. She had joined their class at the start of the year. Luca didn't know much about her. She kept to herself, her head always bent over her work.

Yazmine leaned back in her chair, smiling. Her green eyes were fixed on Zane.

Luca groaned. He could not work out why Zane was so popular. Every boy wanted to be his friend. Every girl had his name written on their pencil case. It made no sense. Zane was a total pain in the butt. He did what he wanted, with no worries about anyone else. Luca was pretty sure Zane didn't even know his name.

Zane was also one of those kids whose phone camera was permanently on selfie mode.

He whipped out his phone now. "Really? I look amazing?" he asked, talking while trying to freeze his snarl.

Yazmine stood up and walked over to the blackboard. "Yeah. Amazingly stupid. Look, I don't know where Ms. Long has gone. But this"—she pointed at the drawing—"must have something to do with us being here. Let's figure it out so we can go eat."

Luca chuckled. This Yazmine was pretty cool.

Zane's frown deepened. "You'd better watch it, new girl."

"Firstly, I've been at this school for six months. I am hardly new," Yazmine retorted, hand on hip. "Secondly, what are you going to do? Pull out your comb and mess up my hair?"

Before Zane could respond, Yazmine turned to Luca. "Zane the Vain will be useless. But I bet you and I can work out what this drawing is. It's a kind of puzzle. You like puzzles, right?"

Luca stared at Yazmine in surprise. How did she know that?

"I guess," he mumbled. "But I don't have any idea what this is. Do you?"

"I think it's a map," she said, tracing the

squiggly line with her finger. "Here's the coastline. And these shapes are landmarks. But the part I can't solve is what country it is."

Yazmine faced the board. Luca and Zane did the same, each tilting their heads to one side as they studied the drawing.

It suddenly dawned on Luca what he was looking at. As he said it aloud, so did Yazmine and Zane.

"Imperia!"

There was a clicking noise. The cabinet at the back of the classroom had somehow unlocked itself! The door swung slowly forward, like a ghost was opening it with an invisible hand. As Luca watched, he knew what was going to happen before it happened, almost like he'd dreamt it.

The Thunder Egg that was always displayed in the cabinet tipped forward. As they watched, it rolled to the edge of the shelf and started to fall. Zane sped across the room and dove toward it. He reached out and caught the egg just before it smashed to the floor.

Luca blinked. He hated to admit it, but that was impressive.

But then Zane pulled a typically Zane move. "Hey, you! Leo or whatever your name is," he called to Luca. "Catch!"

Fear pounded in Luca's chest. "Don't!" he yelled.

But it was too late. The Thunder Egg arced through the air toward him.

Luca leapt up, hands outstretched. As his fingers touched the egg, the classroom lights flickered. Once. Twice. There was a flash of purple. Then everything went black.

Luca was falling. Or was he rising? The air around him felt hot. Hotter than the hottest summer day. It also smelled bad—worse than his dog's breath. Worse than the egg sandwich he found in his bag after vacation.

Luca gasped for breath as he tumbled through the darkness.

THUD!

Luca landed on hard ground. Heat rose

around him. The stink was still there, but it wasn't as strong. Or maybe he was getting used to it?

He sat up. Luca knew he was no longer in Ms. Long's classroom. But where was he? And what was that rumbling noise? As he blinked, the darkness faded and a strange orange glow took its place. Luca peered into the gloom. There was a dark lump nearby. Luca reached out to touch it. It was smooth, warm to the touch, about the size and shape of a football.

The Thunder Egg!

Off in the distance, Luca could see another shape, like a huge mountain. Smoke spewed from the top. Luca's heart thumped. That wasn't a mountain. It was a volcano!

What was going on? He tried to scramble to his feet but fell over. His balance was all wrong.

Someone came toward him through the hazy orange light. Yazmine! Relief flooded through him. He wasn't alone in this place. She looked very small. Had she shrunk? And why was she wearing that weird outfit?

Yazmine was staring at him like he was some kind of monster.

"Yazmine, what on earth—" Luca stopped short.

His voice was harsh, loud. It was like someone had put on a filter to make him sound like a different person. Yazmine stared up at him, mouth half-open in surprise.

Luca tried to stand up again. Once more, he tumbled over. Why couldn't he stand up?

Luca looked down. If he hadn't already fallen over, he would have fallen over now. His limbs had completely changed. His hands and feet were tipped with razor-sharp talons. His body rippled with muscles under a layer of gleaming purple scales. And there was something heavy pulling at his back. Turning, Luca saw he'd grown a massive tail. But that wasn't all. A pair of wings also sprouted from his back. They were folded up, but there was no mistaking them.

"What is going on?" Luca yelled. The words burst from his mouth, along with a plume of fire.

Yazmine took a careful step closer. "Luca? Is that you?"

"Of course it's—" Another plume of fire shot out of his mouth. Luca clapped a hand to his face and scratched himself with a powerful claw.

"Okay, don't freak out when I tell you this," Yazmine said, her voice calm but her eyes bright with wonder. "You are a dragon, Luca."

The ground began to shake. Something big was running toward them. A terrible roar ripped through the smoky air. It sounded like an animal in pain.

Stay calm! Luca told himself. He finally got to his feet without falling. He was so tall!

Luca could see a huge beast lumbering

toward them. It was as wide as a truck. With each step, the ground trembled. As it got closer, Luca saw massive curved claws.

Luca looked down at Yazmine. Should he be protecting her somehow? But Yazmine did not look worried. She had her hands on her hips, a small smile on her face.

The beast was covered in fur. Luca squinted. The fur was purple and very fluffy. Luca's urge to flee vanished. It wasn't possible to be scared of a beast that fluffy. Even if it was huge and ugly.

The creature roared again, showing its big, sharp teeth.

"Get it together, Zane," Yazmine called. "Yelling like that is not going to help."

Luca snorted with laughter. Plumes of smoke shot from his nostrils. *This beast was Zane the Vain?* It made no sense. But at the same time, Luca knew Yazmine was right. Somehow the beast looked like Zane. Was it the hair?

The Zane beast stopped. He crumpled to his knees in front of Luca and Yazmine, squashing a small tree.

"What. Is. Going. On?" Zane moaned.

Yazmine tapped her chin thoughtfully. "I have a theory."

"Right now, I'll take whatever you've got," Luca said.

"I think we are in Imperia," Yazmine said.

Luca felt like he'd been stung by a thousand wasps. "No way! Imperia is just a story made up by Ms. Long."

"I know it sounds impossible," Yazmine said. "It's also impossible to turn into a dragon. Yet look at you. And look at you, Zane. You've become . . . well, you're a hideous monster."

"I don't want to be a hideous monster," Zane whined.

"Don't be such a baby," Yazmine shot back. "Better to be a monster than a tiny human. I get the feeling being big and bulky will be an advantage here. And, hey, you're also very fluffy."

Zane roared. "I DON'T WANT TO BE FLUFFY!"

Luca reached out to touch Zane. "He's as soft as velvet," Luca informed Yazmine. "Could be on a toilet paper commercial."

Zane roared even louder.

Yazmine raised a hand. There was something about the way she did this that made Zane stop roaring and stand up like a well-trained puppy.

"Look," said Yazmine, pointing at the volcano. Thick molten lava oozed out of it. That
was bad enough. But what made it doubly
bad was that the lava had EYES.

And triply bad? It was heading their way.

3

Luca stood glued to the spot, unable to move.

"It's *slithering*," Yazmine muttered.

The lava moved like a snake toward them, gaining speed by the second. They watched as a mouth opened up in the lava. A pair of gleaming fangs appeared. A long, forked tongue flickered in and out. Sparks flew.

It was not a friendly sight.

"The Magma Mamba," Zane whispered, sounding awed.

"How do you know that?" Luca asked, surprise pulling him out of his frozen state.

"It was in one of Ms. Long's stories." Zane shrugged. "I always remember the beasts."

"Seems wise." Yazmine nodded. "I mean, they could be your relations. And they were clearly not just stories."

"Do you remember what Ms. Long said about the Magma Mamba? Or was I the only one paying attention?" Zane asked.

Now that Zane mentioned it, Luca *did* remember their teacher talking about a snake-like monster that lived in volcanoes. Nervous dread began to bubble inside him.

"The one that spits massive fireballs?" he asked.

"Massive *poisonous* fireballs, Luke," Zane corrected him.

"It's Luca, not Luke," Luca pointed out.

Zane wasn't listening.

The enormous snake reared up, its skin roiling like rough seas. Its coffin-shaped head twisted back and forth like it was trying to see something with its beady eyes. All the while its long tongue flickered like a flame.

"Stay very still," Zane whispered. "The Magma Mamba can detect the slightest movement. Ms. Long said it could sense a mouse's fart."

The three of them stood as still as statues.

"As if Ms. Long said *mouse's fart* in class," Yazmine whispered back, trying not to move as she spoke.

Luca held in a laugh.

"How would you know?" Zane hissed. "You don't even remember her talking about it."

"Zane," Yazmine said, "I don't have to remember to know that there is *no way* Ms. Long talked about gassy rodents in class."

Luca did not get involved. Mostly because it was a totally ridiculous argument to be having at any time, let alone with a death-seeking lava snake looming.

But also, something had caught his eye. Nearby grew a sad, scrubby-looking tree.

Dangling from a branch was a single, dried-up leaf.

Luca had a bad feeling about that leaf.

Do not fall! Luca willed it. Maybe dragons had some kind of power over the natural world?

The leaf did not seem to think so. Just as the snake's horrible head swung in their direction, the leaf broke off from the tree. It swirled through the air in a leisurely way, like it was enjoying itself on a sunny day.

As Luca watched in horror, the leaf fluttered toward Yazmine. She looked like she wanted to disappear as the leaf came to rest on her shoulder. Then, suddenly, Yazmine *did* disappear.

"Whaaaat?" Zane gasped.

One minute Yazmine was standing there, a leaf on her shoulder. The next minute, she was gone. But the leaf was still there, hovering in midair.

In a flash, the snake whipped around and lunged toward them. It was so close now, Luca's scales rippled in the heat. The monster opened its jaws, spitting out a huge ball of flame. It shot through the air, crashing into the scrubby tree right next to where Yazmine had been. The tree instantly turned to ash.

Luca blinked. Yazmine was standing next to him again! But before he could say anything, Zane yelled out in alarm.

"It's spotted us. Run!"

Zane turned and bounded off. The snake slithered after him, leaving a trail of scorched earth behind it. It spat out another glowing fireball at Zane.

"DUCK!" Yazmine yelled.

Zane did, just in time. There was a faint smell of singed fur.

Yazmine reached down and picked up the Thunder Egg at Luca's feet. "Let's go while that thing is distracted with Zane."

"You think we should run?" Luca asked. His brain felt thick and foggy. He couldn't keep up with everything that was going on. But he knew one thing: When Zane had ran, the snake had followed.

"Why run when you can fly?" Yazmine

replied. "I'll go on your back with the Thunder Egg. I have a feeling we need to look after it. C'mon!"

"I—I don't know how to fly," Luca stammered.

Everything was happening too fast. He needed time to think, to come up with a plan. That was how Luca always worked through problems.

But there was no time for plans. Zane had dove behind a huge boulder, and now the Magma Mamba had turned back toward them. It was slithering their way!

Yazmine leapt onto Luca's back like she'd been riding dragons her whole life.

"You've got wings," she said through gritted teeth. "My suggestion is you flap them."

Luca gave his wings a flap.

Nothing happened.

"Like you *mean* it, Luca!" Yazmine said, slapping her forehead. "I don't know. Imagine that there's a giant, fireball-spitting snake heading your way?"

Luca took a deep breath. He flapped his wings, harder this time. He rose off the ground before thumping back down. He could feel the heat from the Magma Mamba as it slithered closer.

"Better!" Yazmine cheered. "Maybe you

need a run-up. What about that thing?"

Up ahead was a huge shard of rock angled into the air like a stunt ramp. Luca couldn't even see what was beyond it.

"What if I still can't fly when I get to the end of it?" Luca asked.

"Then we fall," Yazmine said. "And probably break every bone in our bodies. But that won't matter because then we'll be vaporized by a lava snake. So maybe let's go?"

Luca began to gallop. The ground was uneven and littered with rocks. He tripped a few times, righting himself as he picked up speed. He flapped his wings, willing them to lift him high into the air. He rose a few times but always crashed back down a few seconds later.

"You're getting it, Luca!" Yazmine urged, holding tight around his long neck. Luca could hear something in her voice. Fear.

The heat from the Magma Mamba was almost unbearable now. A fireball whizzed past them on the right. Another shot past on the left. It was so close Luca felt a searing burn in one of his wings.

Yazmine yelled at the monster. "You're a lousy shot!"

"Don't taunt it!" Luca groaned.

"Why not? Are you scared I'll make it angry? It's a little late for that."

Desperately, Luca flapped his wings again. He rose into the air and fell back down. Panic gripped him. Maybe he wasn't a flying kind of dragon? Or maybe he couldn't fly with a passenger?

He was on the rocky ramp now. He sped up, but he wasn't at all sure he'd make it to the end. The snake was right behind them!

And then, through the haze, another monster appeared. It was big. It was hairy. It was . . . fluffy.

"Zane!" Luca yelled as he ran. "What are you DOING? You're supposed to be running away!"

"Thought I'd better save you guys," Zane said, passing a paw through the fur on his head in that Zane the Vain way. "Seeing as you're about to be turned into charcoal."

He picked up a massive boulder as if it

weighed no more than a cotton ball. With a bloodcurdling yell, he launched it at the Magma Mamba.

CLUNK!

The boulder hit the snake directly between the eyes. The beast stopped slithering and reared up, hissing smoke into the air.

"Keep running!" Yazmine urged Luca. "We're almost at the end of the ramp. Flap harder than you think you can!"

Luca ran hard up the sloping rock. From the corner of his eye, he saw Zane hefting another boulder skyward. It whistled through the air.

The end of the ramp was in sight.

"C'mon, wings," he muttered. "Don't let me down!"

There was another thud as the rock found its target.

"Bull's-eye!" yelled Zane. "Guys, I think I killed it!"

"Really?" Yazmine yelled over her shoulder.

"Nope, scrap that," yelled Zane again. "I just made it angrier. GET OUT OF HERE!"

Zane turned and ran, the ground vibrating from his heavy feet.

The end of the ramp was three seconds away. Two. One.

Mustering all his strength, Luca leapt off the edge of the ramp, flapping his wings with everything he had.

He began to fall.

"This was a short-lived adventure!" Yazmine yelled in his ear, clinging to his neck.

But then a gust of wind swooped in and lifted them up. They soared away from the edge of the ramp. Away from the volcano. Away from the furious serpent, which now had a massive lump between its eyes.

Luca was doing it. He was actually, unquestionably, without a doubt, FLYING!

"Whoo!" Yazmine yelled, wind whipping through her hair. They were flying higher and higher. "I knew you'd figure it out!"

"Thanks," muttered Luca, pleased and a little embarrassed. "Hey, what happened before? When you, like, disappeared?"

"Disappeared?" Yazmine scoffed. "What are you talking about?"

"When the leaf landed on your shoulder.

One minute you were there, the next you weren't," Luca said. It sounded silly now that he'd said it out loud.

"Seriously?" Yazmine said. "Cool! I did feel a weird tingling. And I definitely *wanted* to be invisible."

"It was only for a few seconds, but it was pretty amazing. Maybe invisibility is your consolation prize."

"Huh?"

"For not being an awesome dragon like me!" Luca laughed, swooping through the air with a roar.

"Careful!" Yazmine snapped, but Luca could hear the smile in her voice. "I'm still babysitting the Thunder Egg back here, remember."

Luca straightened out his flying and looked down. "Wow, check this place out!"

Now that they were away from the volcano, the haze had cleared. Below them sprawled a dense forest, stretching off into the distance. It had a sinister look, with enormous, dark green trees.

Here and there were small clearings, dotted with simple village huts. To the left, Luca could see glimmering ocean. To the right, a mountain range loomed above the trees, the tallest peaks capped with snow. Far off on the horizon was a city of some sort, with towers glittering like tarnished metal.

Luca felt a shiver of excitement. This really was Imperia! He'd imagined the place so clearly as Ms. Long talked about it. But he'd never believed it actually existed. Or that he would get to visit!

Yazmine leaned forward. "Can you see Zane anywhere?"

Luca scanned the forest below. A small, purple dot galloped through the dark trees.

Yazmine gasped.

"What?" Luca asked, immediately on alert.

"The egg," Yazmine said. "It's doing something weird. Look!"

"I'm flying, remember?"

"Just turn your head for a sec," said Yazmine. "You've GOT to see this. It's important. It's not like there's anything to crash into up here."

"Easy for you to say," Luca said, but he

managed to swivel around enough to see the Thunder Egg Yazmine held out.

A line had appeared on the egg's surface. A blue-green light glowed in the groove, like it was lit from within.

Luca checked that they were still going in the same direction as Zane before turning back to look at the geode. The line was now spreading out in all directions, drawing a large, squiggly shape. A purple dot had appeared within the shape, moving along. Another dot was near it, green and also moving. Farther away was a yellow dot. This one was flashing, but not moving.

Yazmine tapped the squiggly line, which had now connected back to where it started.

"It's the same shape as on the blackboard! It's a map of Imperia. I bet we're the green dot."

"What's the purple one, then?" Luca asked.

He and Yazmine filled in the answer together. "Zane!"

"I wonder what the yellow flashing one is," Yazmine mused. She paused, then slapped Luca on the neck as an idea came to her. "I think we're supposed to go to that spot!"

"Can you not whack me whenever you have an idea?" Luca asked. But he had to admit, what Yazmine said made some sense.

"We'd better fly down to talk to Zane," Yazmine said. "He might just keep running and running otherwise."

Luca swooped down toward the trees. He

had no idea how to land, but hopefully he'd figure it out.

"Zane! Hold up!" Yazmine yelled as they drew closer to the huge fluffy beast. Zane kept running. He obviously didn't hear.

Luca tried. "ZANE! STOP!" His voice burst out, so loud and clear that the leaves of the trees trembled and a flock of birds squawked in alarm.

Zane looked up and saw them. He stopped running. Luca swooped down between the trees and skidded to a stop. Not bad for a first landing! Maybe he was getting the hang of this flying business.

Yazmine slid off his back, the Thunder Egg tucked under one arm.

"Is it safe here?" she asked, looking around. "What are those things over there? Do you think they're dangerous?"

She pointed at a group of tiny, wide-eyed creatures hiding in the grass. They were so fuzzy they were practically round.

Zane laughed. "Scared of pom-poms, new girl? They're Fuzzies. I remember Ms. Long talking about them. They are really cute and friendly."

Yazmine ignored Zane and held the Thunder Egg out between them.

Zane took the egg, but instead of looking at the map, he turned it over. On the back of the egg, numbers had appeared.

1:0

"What's that mean?" wondered Luca.

Zane shrugged. "Looks like a scoreboard to me."

Yazmine sighed. "Not everything is a game, you know." She reached over and turned the egg back to the map. "Zane, you might have listened to Ms. Long's stuff about beasts. But I listened to the geography stuff. I used to draw maps as she talked."

Luca had noticed Yazmine bent over her notebook in class. He'd never once thought she was listening, let alone drawing maps!

The drawing on the egg was exactly like the one on the board. There was the outline and there were three shapes: a crown, a tooth, and a fork.

Yazmine tapped the crown. "I think this is King Volcano. I remember Ms. Long talking about it. That's where we started. And see— the yellow light is on the tooth shape. Maybe that's meant to be Wisdom Mountain."

Luca felt a surge of excitement. Wisdom

Mountain featured in a lot of Ms. Long's stories. It was a really important place in Imperia.

"I think I saw it while we were flying," said Yazmine. "It was in the ranges we flew past, the one shaped like a tooth. I say we head there."

Zane frowned. "Hang on. How do we know the egg isn't leading us to another beast?"

Luca shook his head. The moment he'd touched the Thunder Egg, he'd felt goodness within it.

"We can trust it," he said firmly.

There was a sudden noise from the Fuzzies.

The Fuzzies were no longer small and cute.

Now they were red-eyed and enormous. And they were looking at Yazmine in a distinctly hungry way.

"Yaz! Jump on!" Luca yelled.

Yazmine leapt onto Luca's back just as one pounced at her, saliva dripping from its jaws.

Luca roared at the Fuzzies as he rose, sending a plume of fire into the air.

"Yeah, Fuzzies are reeeeeeeally cute and friendly, Zane!" Yazmine called down.

"Sorry, new girl," Zane called back. "I just remembered. Ms. Long also said they like human flesh!"

"Seems like an important detail," Yazmine growled.

"Quit it, you two," Luca said, flapping his

wings as he tried to hover above the ground. "Zane, let's head to Wisdom Mountain. Just look up at me if you need a guide along the way. Hopefully, we can find out what we're doing here. And how on earth we're going to get home."

5

Luca soared above the trees. Yazmine held on to his neck with one hand and the Thunder Egg with the other. As Luca flew toward the mountain range, he zeroed in on one peak that was as white as marble. Yazmine was right. It was definitely tooth shaped. This had to be Wisdom Mountain.

They hadn't gone far when Yazmine let out a yelp. "We're being followed!"

"Yeah, by Zane," Luca said. "He's pretty fast, I have to say."

"Not on the ground," Yazmine said, lowering her voice. "Up here in the sky, just behind us."

Luca swiveled his head around to see a large insect behind them. Its wings whirred at top speed. As it got closer, Luca realized it was not an insect at all. It was a tiny machine, with a sharp point at the front and two propellers at the back. It had two bulging,

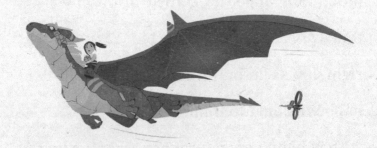

reflective eyes. The machine gave off a nasty buzzing sound.

"What is that thing?" Yazmine muttered.

"A kind of drone?" Luca suggested. "I have to watch where I'm flying, but you keep an eye on it, Yaz."

"I'll keep an eye on it all right," Yazmine said. "But it won't be able to keep an eye on *me*."

Weird thing to say. Luca frowned as he glanced back at Yazmine. What Luca saw made him gasp. Or rather, what he *didn't* see made him gasp.

Yazmine was gone! And so was the Thunder Egg. But Luca could still feel her sitting on his back.

"Um, Yaz?" he said. "Are you invisible again?"

He heard Yazmine chuckle. "Yep! And you know what? Being invisible is just as cool as being a dragon. Let that insect thingy catch up with us so I can have some fun."

Luca slowed his speed. In a flash, the tiny machine zoomed up and hovered alongside them. Its eyes blinked, making a clicking noise.

The eyes are cameras! Luca realized.

Why was this thing taking pictures? Who was spying on them?

Then something very strange happened. The insect lurched sideways like it had been blown by a gust of wind. Then it began shaking up and down. There was a loud crack and the insect split in two. It spluttered and electrical sparks fizzed.

Yazmine reappeared, grinning broadly. In her hand was the crushed machine.

"This won't be bugging us anymore!" Yazmine said. "And look! The numbers on the egg have changed."

The numbers now read: 2:0.

"Nice work, Yaz," said Luca as she dropped the mangled bug pieces into treetops below them.

But Luca felt uneasy. If there was one bug, there was probably more.

The gleaming, toothlike Wisdom Mountain soon rose before them. The sun hit the peak's shiny surface, making it almost too bright to look at. Peering through half-shut eyes, Luca spotted something near the top.

"I can see a cave!" he said.

"Me too," said Yazmine. "The yellow light is flashing like crazy. I think that's where we're meant to go. Hey, remember Ms. Long talking about the Dragon Cave?"

Luca nodded. The Dragon Cave was where the ancient dragons met to talk and share knowledge.

"You think this is it?" he asked.

Yazmine's eyes glimmered with excitement. "Maybe."

Luca slowed as they approached. The area in front of the cave looked smooth and slippery. Stretching out his talons, he touched down, only skidding a little. To his relief, he did not fall over.

"What's that sound?" Yazmine asked as she hopped off Luca's back.

Luca listened. A strange rumbling came from inside the cave. It was soft, but it was somehow fierce as well.

Yazmine shifted the egg from one arm to the other. "Probably another beast wanting to kill us. This place seems to be crawling with them."

There was a rustling from over the edge of the mountain. Luca tensed, ready to take off at short notice.

A huge fluffy paw came into view, followed by another. Zane heaved himself onto the ledge. He was huffing and puffing. "What's going on?" Zane asked, dusting himself off. "Found anything useful?"

"We're not sure if it's useful or deadly." Yazmine shrugged. "There are weird noises coming from that cave."

Luca leaned forward. The rumbling grew louder. This time he could hear words.

DRAGON, HUMAN, BEAST.
STEP INSIDE . . .

With a start, Luca turned to Yazmine and Zane. "Did you hear that?"

Yazmine looked puzzled. "Hear what?"

"That voice, telling us to step inside," Luca said.

"I didn't hear it," said Yazmine. "But come on, let's get in there."

Zane lifted up a paw. "Hang on, new girl. Just because Lewis hears a voice telling us to go into a creepy cave, we all just do it?"

"It's Luca," muttered Luca.

"Not just because of that," Yazmine said. "Look at the egg." It was glowing like a night-light. "It feels like it's pulling me in there. Like it's a magnet being drawn to something."

"Great. How about you go in alone?" Zane

suggested. "You can pull that invisible stunt from earlier."

Yazmine raised an eyebrow. "Are you scared, Zane? A big beast like you?"

"No," Zane retorted. "But if one of us is going to get eaten, it may as well be you. Liam and I can wait out here."

"It's Luca!" Yazmine snapped.

"I'm going in," Luca said, walking toward the cave's entrance. "Coming, Yaz?"

Yazmine grinned. "You bet."

Zane gave a dramatic sigh. "Fine! I'll come, too. If there *are* monsters in there, you two are going to need me."

It was dark in the cave, especially after the dazzling white of the mountain. As their eyes adjusted, they saw a large group of stones on the ground, smooth with age. They were arranged in a perfect circle.

"I think the egg wants me to take it in there," Yazmine said, stepping into the circle. Luca watched, waiting for something to happen.

Nothing.

"Maybe you need to be in here, too?" Yazmine suggested. "Because you're a dragon."

Luca stepped into the circle, carefully tucking his tail in around him.

Still nothing happened.

Yazmine sighed. "Maybe they are just stones. Maybe there's nothing magical about this shape after all."

"Or maybe you just need me in there," Zane said.

"Somehow I doubt—"

As Zane stepped into the circle, everything changed. The Thunder Egg glowed so brightly it lit up the walls of the cave.

Luca, Zane, and Yazmine gasped. Beautiful, intricate drawings covered every inch of the cave's smooth surface.

"Dragons!" Yazmine said, gazing in wonder at the images.

Some of the dragons were seated on thrones. Some were flying. Others were fighting epic battles. The drawings felt like stories. Luca longed to know what they were about.

The rumbling sound grew louder and the

egg glowed ever brighter. A chorus of voices, deep and low, echoed around the cave.

THE FIRST DRAGON HAS RETURNED AND THE GAME HAS BEGUN!

6

Luca turned to the others. "You heard that, right?"

Yazmine and Zane looked at him blankly.

"It just sounds like the wind whistling," Zane said.

"Or far-off thunder," Yazmine added.

WE ARE THE ANCIENT ONES.

DRAGONS WHO DIED LONG AGO.

The voices rumbled.

NOW LISTEN CAREFULLY.

WE HAVE A WARNING FOR YOU

AND YOUR STRANGE FRIENDS.

Luca's heart began to beat very fast.

"What?" Zane asked, running a nervous paw through the fur on his head.

"It's a warning," Luca said. "From, um, long-dead dragons? Called the Ancient Ones. I think they want to help us."

"Call me boring, but I prefer help from things that are still alive," Zane said.

Luca frowned at Zane, signaling him to be quiet. The chorus was speaking again.

THE PROPHECY HAS BEGUN.
YOU ARE PART OF THE GAME NOW.

As Luca repeated the words, Yazmine nodded, her eyes bright in the egg's glow. "So it *is* a game! The numbers on the egg are scores. Zane, you were right."

Zane pumped a furry fist. "YES! Could you say that again but way louder?"

Yazmine rolled her eyes. "Let me get this right. Because we escaped the Magma Mamba and destroyed that insect thingy, we've earned two points?"

Luca nodded as the rumbling voices came once more.

**OUTSIDERS CAN WIN, BUT
ONLY IF YOU WORK TOGETHER.
ALL THREE PLAYERS ARE NEEDED.
AND IF YOU LOSE, ALL OF IMPERIA
WILL PAY THE PRICE.**

Luca passed this on to the others. A doubt gnawed at his mind. Could they work as a team? They were so different. And they didn't get along very well.

Once again, the glow of the egg flared and the cave filled with the rumbling voices.

**BEWARE OF THE ONE WHO NEVER
GREW UP. DARTSMITH. HE LOVES TO
PLAY GAMES BUT HATES RULES. HIS**

LOOKS CHANGE, BUT HIS GOAL STAYS THE SAME: TO WIN AT ANY COST.

Excitement and fear rushed through Luca as he told the others. As he finished, the drawings on the wall faded away. New lines appeared, forming a strange shape. Luca

squinted at it. Was it a jet? As he watched, it began to fly across the surface of the cave.

Yazmine nudged Luca. "Ask them what we need to do."

THE FIRST DRAGON MUST BE RETURNED TO THE CROWN OF FIRE. AND REMEMBER: IT TAKES A DRAGON TO MAKE A DRAGON.

"What did it say?" asked Zane.

Luca repeated the message back, then frowned. "I wonder what the Crown of Fire is?"

"Ask them!" urged Yaz.

But before Luca could, a sudden gust of wind blew into the cave. The strange jet drawing on the cave's wall flickered, then disappeared.

The Thunder Egg stopped glowing. The cave's walls were blank once more.

"Hey, guys," Zane said, stepping out of the stone circle and peering outside. "It looks like a storm's on the way. Being on top of a mountain when it hits is probably a bad idea."

Large, black clouds had formed. A cold wind whipped around the mountain. Luca did not like the idea of trying to fly in a storm.

Yazmine followed Zane to the cave's entrance. She held up the Thunder Egg. A new point of light had appeared on the map etched on the egg's surface. "Maybe this will lead us to the Crown of Fire."

"You two follow the egg's map, and I'll

follow you," Zane bellowed over his shoulder as he headed down the mountain in great strides. "Try to stay below the storm clouds."

Luca gave Zane a moment to get ahead before launching off the side of Wisdom Mountain, Yazmine on his back once more.

The wind was getting stronger by the second, tossing Luca about like a leaf.

"I can't see Zane," he called to Yazmine. "How far until we reach the spot on the map?"

"Yeah, about that," Yazmine yelled over the thunder. "We might have a slight problem."

Luca looked back as lightning lit up the sky. He only saw the map for a split second. Lines looped all over the surface in a mad tangle, flashing on and off.

"This is one scrambled egg," Yazmine declared. "The electrical storm must be messing it up."

"I'd better land," Luca called.

Rain lashed them as Luca fought his way through the wild winds. By the time his talons touched the muddy earth, he was exhausted.

"I really hope a deadly beast doesn't choose this moment to appear." Yazmine groaned as they collapsed into the mud.

As it happened, a beast did choose that exact moment to appear. But it was a familiar beast. Zane looked like an oversize stuffed toy that had been left out in the rain.

"Good to see you survived," Zane said. He shook himself like a dog at the beach until his fur looked normal again. "I didn't think you two would cope with that storm."

"I didn't think your fur would cope with that storm," Yazmine retorted.

Luca stood up and looked around. He was tired and hungry and in no mood for these two sniping at each other.

He turned and spotted something so surprising that he thought he might be imagining it. A wooden building, its windows glowing cheerfully! Above the front door hung a sign:

INN
ALL CREATURES WELCOME

Luca blinked, half expecting the building to disappear.

"What are you blinking at?" Zane asked,

swinging around. He pounded toward the front door the moment he saw the inn.

Yazmine looked at Luca. "Coming?"

"It could be a trap," Luca pointed out.

"It probably *is* a trap," Yazmine agreed. "But I'm so wet and hungry, I don't think I care." She followed Zane.

Still Luca hesitated.

The delicious smell of hot food wafted his way. Luca's stomach gurgled loudly. Trap or not, he couldn't resist a moment longer!

7

Zane pushed open the inn door. A wave of warmth, chatter, and cheerful music floated out. The place was filled with an assortment of humans and beasts. Luca scanned the crowd, hoping to see another dragon. Then he remembered: All the dragons were long gone from Imperia.

Everyone stopped talking and turned to stare. They were not staring at Yazmine. They were not staring at the fluffy Zane beast. They were staring at Luca. He hated being the center of attention. Unfortunately, it was hard for a dragon to melt into the background. Luca was glad that scales did not blush.

Zane was perfectly at ease having all eyes on him. "Hi, guys! How are you all?" he called cheerily, as if he were walking into the locker room before football practice.

"Look, there's space over there," Yazmine said, leading them to a spare table.

There was a human-sized chair and a much wider one with sturdy legs, clearly meant for beasts. There was room beside the table for Luca to sit, too.

Yazmine tucked the Thunder Egg under the

table on the floor next to Luca. "Keep an eye on it, everyone," she said. "If we lose the egg, we'll never figure out how to get Luca to that Crown of Fire."

Luca held up a paw. "Hang on. You think *I* am the dragon that needs returning to the fire?"

Yazmine and Zane looked at him as if he'd just said the silliest thing in the world. "Dude, you're a dragon," Zane said.

"I know that! But I'm not the one in the prophecy." He paused, thinking. "Am I?"

Yazmine shrugged. "I haven't seen any other dragons around, have you?"

A man appeared with a huge tray. Balanced on top of it were three servings of food.

"Welcome, Outsiders. I have one human dinner here. And for the first time in years, one dragon dinner," he said, looking at Luca like he was some sort of miracle. He placed meals in front of Yazmine and Luca. "And this one's for the fluffy beast," the man added, handing a large bowl to Zane.

Yazmine stared at the food. "Thanks, but we haven't ordered anything."

"Compliments of a fellow customer," the waiter said, turning to leave. "Enjoy your meals."

"That seems unlikely," Zane muttered.

Yazmine's food didn't look too bad. It was some sort of pizza. But Luca's own bowl contained little more than a kind of multicolored swirling fog. And Zane's looked terrible! He'd been given a bowl filled with gross-looking brown lumps swimming in an acid-green liquid. It smelled of dirty socks and old cheese.

"There's no way I can eat this." Zane pushed away his bowl.

"Have some of my pizza," Yazmine said. "It's really tasty."

But when Zane took a bite, he made a face. "Are you kidding? That's awful!"

Luca looked down at his own bowl. It looked weird but smelled surprisingly good. He just had no idea how to eat it.

"It's Dragon Mist. You breathe it in," said a voice.

A tall, thin boy walked toward them. He had

a dark woolen cape slung around his shoulders. The hood partly covered his face. Luca could just make out the glimmer of blue eyes and a sharply pointed nose.

The boy smiled. "Try it," he urged Luca. "This inn was known for its Dragon Mist back in the day. Clearly, they haven't forgotten the recipe. And the Beast Slop is apparently excellent," he added, looking at Zane.

To Luca's surprise, Zane skewered one of the lumps on a claw and nibbled it. His eyes widened. "It's AMAZING!"

Luca leaned over his bowl of Dragon Mist and allowed one of the tendrils of fog to waft into his nostrils. Instantly, Luca felt as if hot chocolate was slipping down his throat, warming his belly. He took another breath, deeper this time, and felt his energy returning.

The caped boy watched them carefully. "So! You are Outsiders, yeah?"

"You could say that," Zane snorted. Green goop dribbled down his chin.

Yazmine shot him a warning look. "We're travelers," she said in a polite, careful voice. "Speaking of which, we'd better get going."

"No hurry," said the boy, pulling up a chair. "It's still pouring out there. I noticed you have a Thunder Egg with you. Do you realize it's nearly ready to hatch? You'll want to get rid of it before that happens."

Luca, Yazmine, and Zane stared at the boy

in shock. Yazmine was the first to recover the powers of speech.

"Are you telling me that there is a *baby* inside this rock?" she said.

The boy laughed. "Of course! A baby dragon. What did you think was in it? Chocolate? Back in the dragon days, there used to be lots of those around. But Imperia hasn't seen one in years. Frankly, I'd like to keep it that way."

Luca felt his pulse quicken. "Why?"

"Dragons used to rule Imperia. That was not a good time." The boy sighed dramatically. "Don't get me wrong. I don't have a problem with dragons personally. Some of my best friends were dragons. But they did not make good leaders. Imperia was a complete mess while they were in charge. But Dartsmith is our ruler now, and he's looking after us all very well."

Luca, Yazmine, and Zane exchanged glances. This was the exact opposite of what Ms. Long had told them.

The boy kept talking. "Dartsmith has asked us all to keep an eye out for Thunder Eggs. To prevent the place becoming overrun with dragons again. What are you planning to do with this one?"

"We were told by a bunch of dead dragons to take it to a fire," Zane said, chewing noisily on another lump.

Luca flinched. This felt like private information. Besides, there was something odd
about this boy.

The boy leaned forward. "That's not a good
idea," he said. "This egg needs to be destroyed.
And the only way to do that is to feed it to the
Magma Mamba. It's a giant snake that guards
King Mountain."

"Oh, we've met," said Zane grimly.

"Then I am sure you don't want to go anywhere near it again," the boy said kindly.
"How about you give the egg to me and I'll
feed it to the beast? I'm not afraid."

"No, thanks," Yazmine said firmly. "The
Thunder Egg stays with us."

Luca nodded. There was a lot he didn't understand about Imperia yet. But he was certain they needed to protect the egg.

The boy stood up abruptly, his chair crashing to the ground. His blue eyes clouded over like the stormy skies outside.

"Then you are even more foolish than you look," he hissed, swooshing his cape open.

A cloud of buzzing insects appeared out of the cape's folds. They were just like the mini drone that had followed them earlier! But this time there was a lot of them.

The insects swarmed around Luca, Yazmine, and Zane, jabbing at them with their needle-sharp spikes. Yazmine grabbed a chair and swung wildly at them. Zane jumped up and down, crushing the little machines beneath his massive paws.

Luca swatted them with his powerful wings, knocking over a nearby table as he did so.

It did not take long for the three of them to deal with the swarm. But it was long enough. By the time they stopped to take a breath and look around, the boy had vanished. And that wasn't all.

Yazmine let out a groan. "The Thunder Egg! It's gone!"

8

The tavern door slammed shut. Luca, Yazmine, and Zane looked at one another, and then raced for the exit.

Outside, the rain had stopped but the wind howled louder than ever. Night had fallen and the woods were veiled in darkness.

Through the trees, Luca spotted a light floating in midair.

"Look! The Thunder Egg!" he cried.

As Luca's eyes adjusted, he saw the egg wasn't floating. The boy was running into the woods with it. Glancing back, the boy caught sight of the trio.

He stopped and held up the egg, a triumphant smile on his face. The scoreboard had reappeared on the egg's surface, but the numbers had changed:

2:1

Luca groaned. "And we just lost that round."

Yazmine looked grim. "No wonder. We just lost the egg."

"Don't worry about that," Zane said. "What is he up to?"

The boy's thick cloak had flared out. Then it began to fold, as if an invisible hand was doing origami with it. The dart-like mechanical insects swarmed around as his cloak reshaped into streamlined wings that resembled a fighter jet.

The boy zoomed high into the air. With the sound of an engine accelerating, he disappeared from sight, like an arrow shot from a bow.

An arrow? Something clicked for Luca. "That was no ordinary boy. That was Dartsmith!"

"The ruler of Imperia?" Zane sounded doubtful. "How come no one recognized him in the inn?"

"His looks change, but his goal stays the same," Luca chanted, recalling the rumbling voices from the cave.

"Of course!" said Yazmine, slapping her forehead. "Ms. Long said he was a master of disguise. Who knows what he normally looks like." She leapt up onto Luca's back. "Quick! After him!"

"I'm on it," Zane called, pounding into the dark woods.

Luca took off. Flying at a low level was harder than flying above the tree line. He could not let his focus slip for a moment. When the gap between the trees was too narrow, Luca tipped to the side. He had no time to warn Yazmine, but luckily she held on tight.

Dartsmith, powered by his jetlike cloak, was incredibly fast. He darted between the trees with ease. Luca, who was much bigger, was in constant danger of slamming into tree trunks. To make things even harder, his wings kept getting caught in vines and branches. Each time they got snagged, he had to waste valuable seconds pulling himself free.

"We're going uphill," Yazmine called above the wind. "Also, um . . ." She trailed off.

"What is it?" Luca asked. He was not in the mood for more bad news.

"I think we're about to see our old friend the Magma Mamba again."

The volcano loomed up ahead, belching red lava against the night sky. Luca caught a whiff of the eggy smell.

Luca's insides flipped. He fought to keep himself calm. They had to stay focused. There was no room for mistakes now. If Dartsmith fed the Thunder Egg to the snake, they would lose. Luca had a feeling that if they lost, they wouldn't be able to get home. Winning a game had never mattered so much to Luca in his life.

"We can do this, Luca," Yazmine urged. "Because we've got something that Dartsmith lacks. We've got one another."

Luca would have laughed at that at the start of this adventure. But now he realized it was true. They were kind of a team. The thought gave him a surge of energy.

The higher they went, the scrubbier the trees became. Luca thought this might make the flying easier, but the reverse was true.

Small scrubby trees were even harder to fly around! The tree branches clutched at Luca's wings as he and Yazmine whipped past. It felt like they were deliberately trying to slow him!

Dartsmith's words swirled in Luca's head. *Dragons don't make good leaders.* Was everyone in Imperia against dragons? Even the trees? But Ms. Long always said that Imperia would only find peace when the three dragons returned.

Luca frowned. He'd only been a dragon for a few hours. But already he knew what a dragon's heart was like. He felt the goodness of those ancient creatures pulsing in his veins. Dragons being bad leaders just didn't ring true.

Up ahead, Dartsmith came into view, doing midair loops.

"What a show-off," muttered Yazmine.

"I wouldn't come any closer if I were you," Dartsmith called. "The Magma Mamba has been feeding on lava. It's bigger and stronger than ever. But it has plenty of room left for the Thunder Egg. Better get going while you can, Outsiders."

"We're not going anywhere until we get the Thunder Egg back!" Yazmine yelled.

"That's just not going to happen," sneered the boy. "Thunder Eggs are a rare treat for the Magma Mamba. And it will make it stronger than ever. There'll be no new dragons in Imperia while I am in charge!"

Out of the darkness, the Magma Mamba rose up, swaying from side to side. It glowed red-hot and huge against the night sky.

Luca gulped. The snake had doubled in size! Its tongue flicked in and out, as long and wide as a highway.

"Watch out!" Zane called as the hideous creature opened its jaws and sent a fiery venom ball their way.

Luca swerved and the ball shot past them.

It crashed into a group of trees, the whole patch of forest immediately exploding.

The snake reared into strike position and opened its jaws once more. Luca could feel the heat reflecting off his scales. Yazmine ducked low on his back.

Dartsmith flew toward the giant snake. "You can have those three in a moment," he promised it. "But first, look what I've got for you!"

He held up the glowing Thunder Egg. The snake hissed and opened its jaws wider. Burning venom dripped from its huge, gleaming fangs.

"STOP!" Luca roared, filling the air with plumes of green smoke.

"Try and stop me," Dartsmith said, mocking him.

Luca flew toward the snake as fast as he could. At the same time, Dartsmith zoomed up. Propelled by his army of insect drones, he was superfast. He hovered dangerously close to the jaws of the giant snake.

"Dinnertime!" Dartsmith sang, and he tossed the Thunder Egg into the air.

The egg spun high into the night sky, pausing for a split second before it began tumbling down.

"Catch it!" Yazmine yelled desperately.

Luca surged forward with speed he didn't know he had. But a nearby tree grabbed at him, clawing at his wings, holding him back.

It's no good, thought Luca.

But then something shot up into the air. Something big. Something strong. Something fluffy!

"Go, Zane!" Yazmine cheered as Zane leapt into the air, stretching out his massive, furry paws.

Dartsmith let out a furious cry and darted toward the egg, too.

"They're all going to crash!" Yazmine gasped.

Just as the snake's burning fangs went to close in around the egg, two big fluffy paws pulled it away.

"Got it!" Zane yelled as he knocked into

Dartsmith midair, sending the boy hurtling away.

"Noooooo!" Dartsmith screamed. His cloak-jet collapsed, and he tumbled down, head over heels. He disappeared into the darkness with one final screech. "The game isn't over yet!"

Zane landed expertly, the egg tucked into one hairy armpit. "That takes care of Dartsmith. For now, at least," he said. Zane looked at the egg and then back up at the others. "You know, I've had a thought."

"So have I," Yazmine said. Luca swerved and Yazmine ducked to avoid an incoming fireball. "Ever since Dartsmith told us the egg was a dragon ready to hatch."

Zane nodded. "So maybe THIS"—he held up the Thunder Egg—"is the first dragon in the prophecy? The one that needs returning to the fire?"

The snake spotted the egg and swooped toward Zane, who leapt out of the way.

"Exactly!" whooped Yazmine. "You don't look very smart. But, Zane, you sure have your moments."

Zane grinned at Yazmine. "High praise coming from you. You two distract the grumpy snake. I'll handle the rest."

Luca turned to Yazmine. "How exactly do we distract an angry lava snake?"

Yazmine looked excited. "What have we got that the snake hasn't?"

"Our tempers under control?"

Yazmine laughed. "That, plus wings and invisibility. We can outfly it and we can totally confuse it. I say we split up. I'll go help Zane with the egg."

Luca nodded. "I'll keep the snake busy, then," he said, trying to sound braver than he felt. "My first goal is to stop it from turning Zane into a lump of coal."

"And my first goal," Yazmine said with a grin, "is to disappear."

With that, Yazmine vanished. All Luca could hear was the faint sound of human feet running away.

Yaz's voice floated through the gloom. "Good luck, Luca! We can win this game, I just know it."

With a mighty flap, Luca shot into the air. "Hey, you! Overgrown glowworm!" he roared loudly.

He swooshed as close to the beast's head

as he dared, feeling his scales crackle in the extreme heat.

The snake hissed in fury and struck out at him. Luca swerved out of the way just in time.

How were the others doing? Glancing down, Luca saw Zane running along the base of the volcano. But the egg was nowhere in sight!

"Zane!" he called in alarm. "Where's the egg?"

"Don't worry," Zane called. "Yaz's got it. She's right here, running next to me. Turns out when she's holding the egg, it disappears, too."

Yazmine's voice floated up from below. "Luca, we're going to drop the egg into the volcano. That *must* be the Crown of Fire, right?"

But as Yazmine spoke, something terrible happened. Yazmine—and the egg—became visible again.

Unfortunately, the Magma Mamba also noticed. It prepared to pounce.

"Yazmine!" Luca roared. "We can see you! Throw the egg back to Zane. Quick!"

Luca flew at the snake again, hoping to draw its attention away from Zane and the Thunder Egg.

"Over here, snakey-snake!" he roared.

The snake whipped around and set its beady eyes on Luca once more.

Luca's mind raced. Were they really meant

to throw the precious Thunder Egg into the volcano? They had worked so hard to protect it! He couldn't shake the feeling he was forgetting something.

There was a thud below. In horror, Luca saw that Zane had fallen and the egg had slipped from his hands. It was flying through the sky.

Quick as a flash, Yazmine leapt up to grab it. As her hands wrapped around it, both she and the egg vanished again.

Clearly Yazmine's invisibility wasn't very stable. Luca wondered if it was because she was running. Or maybe it was something to do with the egg? Either way, they couldn't keep this up for long.

"Watch out!" Zane yelled.

Luca darted away just in time to avoid a venom ball speeding past.

"Throw the egg into the volcano," Luca called down. He was surprised by how sure he sounded. It wasn't how he felt.

With a nod, Zane started leaping up the side of the volcano. The beast sure could run!

Right, thought Luca. *Time to put this snake out of action.*

Luca whipped past its coffin-shaped head. "Catch me if you can, you legless lizard!"

Hissing, the snake struck out at him angrily. Luca dodged, then wheeled around again, dive-bombing the snake.

A plan was forming in his head. It was a

pretty strange one. But maybe it would work.

"Catch me if you can!" he taunted again.

He began flying in and out of the snake's coils. Back and forth, around and around, up and down. Luca flew every which way, leading the snake through its own loops.

In the corner of his eye, Luca saw that Zane had reached the rim of the volcano. Yazmine reappeared by Zane's side, holding the Thunder Egg.

"You're the football champ," Yazmine called, lightly tossing Zane the egg. "You should be the one to throw it. But don't mess up!"

Zane raised the egg high above his head. Luca took a deep breath as he watched. This was it! With all his beastie might, Zane hefted it into the bubbling lava.

Immediately a huge plume of smoke shot out of the volcano, the Thunder Egg right in the middle of it!

Zane leapt up toward the egg and caught it yet again. "Got it!"

"You stupid volcano!" Yazmine yelled. "Why did you spit out the egg?"

Luca couldn't help laughing. "Only you would get mad at a volcano, Yaz," he said. "Hold on! Incoming fireball!"

"It's so frustrating!" Yazmine complained. "This has GOT to be the fire they were talking about. *The first dragon must be returned to the Crown of Fire,* right?"

It was then that something dawned on Luca. "Hold on!"

"What?" asked Yazmine.

"*I* have to do it," said Luca. "The voices in the cave said, *It takes a dragon to make a dragon.* Maybe I have to be the one to drop the egg in? So it can hatch?"

Yazmine and Zane considered this for a moment. Then they nodded.

"Makes sense," said Zane.

"Absolutely. I'll distract the snake while you do the throwing," Yazmine called.

Luca grinned. "No need. Our snake's a little, um, tied up at the moment."

Everyone looked over at the Magma Mamba. It was now a furious, writhing knot of lava.

"You've tied the snake into a little bow!" Zane looked impressed.

"Strictly speaking, it tied itself up." Luca chuckled. "Throw me the egg?"

Luca swooped lower as Zane threw the Thunder Egg high into the air. The egg flew in a perfect arc toward Luca. It really was handy having a football star around.

The egg spun in the air and then began to fall.

"Catch it, Luca!" Zane yelled.

Luca swooped forward to grab it, grinning. "You finally learned my name!"

"What are you talking about?" Zane scoffed. "I've always known your name. Now, are you going to get that final goal or not?"

Luca wrapped his claws tightly around the Thunder Egg. "You bet!"

Luca soared up until he was directly above the volcano. All he could see was lava bubbling, red and hot. On the edge of the volcano were Zane and Yaz, looking up at him.

Here goes! Luca thought, releasing his grip on the precious egg.

The Thunder Egg plummeted into the molten lava. Had Luca's heart stopped beating? It felt like it!

Instantly, the lava changed from red to a swirling golden yellow. Then it began to drain away like someone had pulled the plug. There was something at the volcano's base.

Luca peered down. It was a golden nest! Now nestled safely in it was the Thunder Egg.

Yazmine stretched her arms out wide. "Whoooo! We did it!"

Words flashed on the egg.

Round one complete.

A rumble of thunder sounded all around them. Luca felt himself being sucked into the volcano. He saw a flash of purple as Zane and Yazmine were also sucked in.

Down they went, tumbling over and over. Just before Luca hit the molten sea, darkness closed in around him.

Luca landed heavily. He slowly opened his eyes and sat up. He was back in Ms. Long's classroom. The roar of a lava-filled volcano was replaced with the sound of kids playing outside at lunchtime.

Yazmine and Zane were also picking themselves up, looking dazed. Zane was no longer a beast, and Yazmine was back in her normal clothes. All the mud and mess of their adventure had vanished.

Looking down, Luca saw that he, too, had returned to his human form. He wasn't sure how he felt about that. It was good to be back in his regular skin. But he was going to miss those wings! The talons had been cool, too.

"Well, that was . . . intense," Yazmine said, brushing her clothes off. "How long have we been gone?"

Luca felt for his phone. It was in his pocket, as usual. "You're not going to believe this," he gasped. "We've only been gone a few minutes."

"I guess time passes differently in Imperia." Yazmine shrugged.

A sudden wave of doubt hit Luca. "Did that . . . really happen?"

"Of course it happened," Zane said, fixing his hair. "All three of us were there. Besides, I do not have the imagination to come up with something as wild as that on my own."

"I wonder if we'll go back again?" Yazmine wondered.

Zane stared at her in disbelief. "We'll definitely be going back. We're part of it now. Part of the biggest, most important game ever. That egg was only the first dragon. Round one. I bet it will get even harder from here."

Luca let this sink in. It kind of made sense.

"But that Dartsmith dude doesn't stand a chance against us three." Zane went on. "Luca, you were an awesome dragon."

"Hey, thanks, man." Luca was prouder than he wanted to let on.

"And, Yazmine—wow! I mean, you were one step ahead of the game the whole time," Zane continued.

"You were the best beast I've ever worked with," Yazmine said, like Zane was only one of the many beasts she had been on adventures with.

"I was pretty epic, wasn't I?" Zane grinned, running his hand through his hair again. "Being a beast was pretty cool. I just hope I am a little less fluffy next time."

"Really?" Yazmine chuckled. "Because I'm kind of hoping you'll be fluffier."

"So what do we do now?" wondered Luca.

"I don't know about you, but I'm going to go play football." Zane strode across the room. "My team will be wondering where I am. My *other* team, that is."

Before Zane could reach the door, Ms. Long opened it. "Time's up! I hope it wasn't too boring in here?" A tiny smile twitched at the corner of their teacher's mouth.

Thousands of questions swelled inside Luca. He didn't know where to begin.

Luckily, Yazmine did. "Ms. Long! Why didn't you tell us that Imperia was real?"

"Imperia?" repeated Ms. Long slowly, like she only half remembered the name. "From my stories? Well, I never said it *wasn't* real, did I?"

Luca glanced at Yaz and Zane. It was clear Ms. Long was not going to give away very much.

He looked around the room. Luca felt sick. The other two Thunder Eggs weren't there! Had they been stolen?

Ms. Long saw where Luca was looking. "The remaining two geodes have been moved for safekeeping. But they'll turn up again. Whenever they are needed."

Needed for what? Luca longed to ask.

But Ms. Long glanced at her watch impatiently. "Right! Outside, you three! You all need exercise before class starts."

Luca could hardly believe it. He had been flying through storms and getting a monstrous lava snake to tie itself in knots. Surely that was enough exercise for one day!

But there was no point arguing. Ms. Long might have a strange connection to the mysterious, magical realm of Imperia, but she was also a teacher. And all teachers were obsessed with kids getting fresh air and exercise.

"Ms. Long," Yazmine asked. "Will you need

us to stay back during lunch again?"

Ms. Long tilted her head to the side. "That depends if you are willing to. I know that my classroom can be a slightly . . . strange place at times."

"It's definitely strange," Yazmine agreed. "But we're up for it, aren't we?" She turned to Zane and Luca.

"Absolutely," said Zane, without hesitation. "We're a team now. The best team."

Luca grinned and nodded. They were a weird team, no doubt about it. *But sometimes*, he decided, *weird works*.

DRAGON GAMES

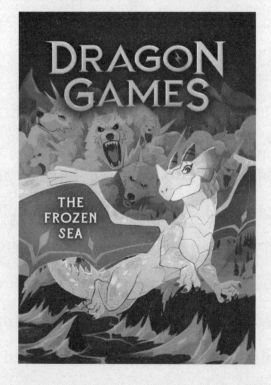

Turn the page for a special sneak peek of

Dragon Games #2: *The Frozen Sea*!

"Luca, Yazmine, and Zane. Come to my desk immediately!"

Luca sat up with a jolt. He had completely zoned out. Had Ms. Long noticed? Probably. She was the kind of teacher who always seemed to know exactly what was going on. But surely Ms. Long would understand why Luca was distracted. After all, how often did you discover the imaginary place your teacher always talked about—Imperia—was not imaginary at all?

He'd found this out when he, Yazmine, and Zane were suddenly transported to Imperia! In Imperia, Luca had turned into a flying, fire-breathing dragon. Zane had become a beast—one that was super big, super strong, and super fluffy. Yazmine had stayed in human form but had the power to become invisible.

At school, the three of them were not friends. In fact, they barely spoke to one another. But in Imperia, they'd become a team. Their first task had been to battle with a massive lava snake called the Magma Mamba, and safely deliver the Thunder Egg into the Crown of Fire—in a volcano!

They'd been through a lot. It was hard to go back to normal after such a big adventure.

As Luca stood up, he glanced over at Yazmine. She shrugged, a smile twitching at the corners of her mouth. She did not look worried. In fact, her eyes sparkled with excitement. Luca's heart thumped as a new thought crossed his mind. Maybe they weren't in trouble. Maybe they were going back to Imperia!

They had completed the first task. But where there's a *first task* there's always more! Luca knew there were two other Thunder Eggs to return. That meant two more rounds of this dangerous game they were playing.

Luca, Yazmine, and Zane all arrived at

Ms. Long's desk at the same time. It was clear from the grin on Zane's face that he, like Yazmine, was confident they weren't in trouble.

"So, Ms. Long," Zane said, grinning as he ran his fingers through his hair. "Have you got a *task* for us? Is there somewhere *special* you want us to go?"

Zane was either incredibly brave or incredibly foolish to speak to Ms. Long like this. It was sometimes a little hard to tell with Zane.

Ms. Long fixed Zane with a stony stare that made him wilt.

"Yes, Zane," she said. "I do have a job for you three. I need you to go to the gym and clean up the equipment room. The gym teacher tells me that your class left it in a terrible mess."

Ms. Long turned back to the rest of the class.

"What?" Zane protested. "That's not fair! We—"

Yazmine grabbed Zane by the arm and pulled him out of the classroom. Luca followed close behind.

"We dealt with that snake in Imperia," Zane grumbled. "And we beat Dartsmith at his own game. She should be treating us like heroes! But no. We're being punished!"

"Don't you get it?" Yazmine asked, leading the way down the empty hallways toward the gym. "We're probably going back to Imperia right now. I bet when we open the door to the equipment room, we'll be transported back there!"

Zane went quiet. Luca felt a rush of adrenaline. What Yazmine said made total sense!

The gym was empty when they arrived. The trio made their way over to the equipment room at the back.

"Let me open it!" Zane said. He made a face at the others as he turned the door handle. Slowly, the door pushed back, revealing . . .

A very messy room full of sports equipment.

Luca's heart sank. Zane looked crushed, too. But Yazmine just shrugged. "No use getting upset about it."

Even so, Luca could tell she was disappointed as well.

In the back corner stood a metal cage where all the balls were kept. There were footballs and soccer balls, volleyballs and basketballs. But the trapdoor at the front of the cage was open and the balls had spilled out all over the floor.

Yazmine waded her way through them and shut the metal trapdoor. "Let's get this job done," she said, pushing up her sleeves and bending low.

They quickly got a good rhythm going. Luca scooped up a ball and passed it to either Yazmine or Zane. Yazmine dropped the balls into the cage. Zane, being Zane, used it as a chance to practice his basketball skills. He jumped as high as he could to toss the balls into the cage.

As the room started to clear, Luca noticed

funny marks on the floor. There was something about the shape they made . . .

"Hey!" he called to the others. "Does this look familiar?"

Zane stared at the squiggly lines emerging on the floor. "It's just like the map that was on the blackboard before we went to Imperia last time."

"You're right! There's Wisdom Mountain," Yazmine said, pointing to a toothlike shape in the middle. "And there's the inn and the Crown of Fire. All the places we went to! But hang on . . . what's this?"

Yazmine kicked aside a basketball near the top of the map. Luca squinted at it. *Was it a house? A palace?* It was surrounded by dots that looked a bit like snowflakes. Or insects? Luca shivered. Maybe they were Dartsmith's army of insect drones. They had been hard to battle last time.

Luca bent down to pick up another ball. The moment he touched it, he knew it was special. It was oddly shaped, and its surface was rough.

"Guys," he said, holding it up. "I think I've found a Thunder Egg!"

"Can I look?" asked Zane. He took it from Luca and inspected it. "It's not the same as the last one. This one's smaller and lighter in color. Maybe it's a different type of dragon? And it's cold."

"I'm not surprised it's cold," Yazmine said. "It's covered in snow."

Luca and Zane stared at her. "What are you talking about? There's no snow on it. How could there be? It's the middle of summer!"

"You can't see it? How very interesting." She stretched out her hands. "Zane, pass it to me?"

Zane did as she asked. The moment Yazmine's hands touched the egg, the sports equipment room—and everything in it—vanished.

ABOUT THE AUTHORS

Maddy Mara is the pen name of Australian creative duo Hilary Rogers and Meredith Badger. Hilary is a writer and former publisher; Meredith is a writer, and teaches English as a second language. Together they have written or created many bestselling series for kids. Their most recent series is the Dragon Girls, which has over a million copies in print, and is available in multiple countries and languages. They both currently live in Melbourne, Australia. Their website is maddymara.com.